E   Alden, Laura.
ALD   Halloween safety

           93007633 /AC

Halloween Safety

by Laura Alden
illustrated by Jodie McCallum

created by Wing Park Publishers

 CHILDRENS PRESS ®
CHICAGO

Library of Congress Cataloging-in-Publication Data

Alden, Laura, 1955-
    Halloween safety / by Laura Alden ; illustrated by Jodie
McCallum.
        p.   cm. — (Circle the year with holidays)
    "Created by Wing Park Publishers."
    Summary: Joey and Rachel enjoy trick-or-treating on
Halloween and almost lose their bags of goodies.
    ISBN 0-516-00684-3
    [1. Halloween—Fiction.]   I. McCallum, Jodie, ill.   II. Title.
III. Series.
PZ7.A3586Hal   1993
[E]—dc20   93-7633
                                                         CIP
                                                         AC

Halloween Safety

Finally, it was Halloween. I was a skeleton.
Rachel was a witch. And our little brother Ethan
was a pumpkinhead.

"BOO!" I said to the pumpkinhead. He just
laughed.

"Joey," said Mom. "Stop that and listen to
me. It's time for trick-or-treating.

"Dad is not home yet. He will be here soon. But, Rachel, Joey and you can go out together.

"Now, both of you, remember the rules. First, only go to friends' homes. Second, hold hands and look both ways when you cross the street. Third, say 'thank you' for the treats!"

"BOO!—THANK YOU!" I said.

Ethan laughed again.

HALLOWEEN RULES

1. Go only to friends.
2. Hold hands and look both ways.

Say
THANK YOU!

Mom knelt down to hug us. "More safety rules," she said. "First, keep your white mittens on, Joey. And Rachel, wear this white scarf. White will help drivers see you when it gets dark. Now, go on," she said. "And don't trip over any jack-o'-lanterns!"

"Let's go," I said, running out the door.

"Walk!" called Mom.

So we walked to the house next door.

"Trick-or-treat!" said Rachel.

"BOO!" I said.

"Hmmm...pretty scary," said Mr. Burns. "But you look a little like Joey and Rachel."

I rattled my chain. Mr. Burns dropped candy into our bags.

"Thank you," we said.

We went to lots more houses and got lots more treats. One lady gave us caramel apples. Another gave us jack-o'-lantern muffins.

We passed ghosts, and black cats, and a big scarecrow!

I moved closer to Rachel when we passed
a big witch.

Soon we came to Mrs. Kline's house. She is Mom's friend. She invited us in to get warmed up—and to have popcorn and apple cider.

"Mmmm, good!"

After a little while, Mrs. Kline said, "It's getting dark. You had better go home now."
"Thanks, Mrs. Kline," we said.

We turned on our flashlights and headed for home. I shined my light into my bag to look at all the candy.

Then, out of the corner of my eye, I saw
a shadow move toward us in the trees.

"Something's following us," I whispered.

"Stop it, Joey. You're such a scaredy-cat," Rachel said.

"No really, look!" I said, shining my flashlight into the trees.

But the shadow had disappeared. I rattled my chain anyway and we kept walking.

Suddenly Rachel stopped. I stopped.

"I saw it," she said, grabbing my hand. "Come on. Walk faster."

We were almost home.

"Let's run!" I said. We ran
down the sidewalk,
up onto the porch,
through the door—
SAFE!

"Someone's following us!" I shouted.
Mom was right there. We ran into her arms.

"What did you see?" she asked. "Are you
sure it wasn't only—"

"Me," said Dad's voice from the doorway. "I didn't mean to scare you," he said.

"You tricked us!" Rachel said.

Dad winked at me. "I got home just after you left. And I wanted to make sure you were being careful," he said.

23

"I'm glad you were close to home when you saw a stranger," said Mom, smiling, "even if it wasn't a stranger—but was just Dad. Now I think you deserve some of those treats you brought home. But first I'll look through them to be sure they are all O.K. Where are your bags?"

We looked around. Our bags were gone! Then we heard Ethan giggling.

"After the pumpkinhead!" I yelled. "He has our bags!"

"Tricked again!" Rachel shouted, running after me.

But now we were laughing, too.

27

Activity Pages

Safety Activities

1. Using the story, make and discuss a trick-or-treating safety list. Points to include:

• If you are going at night, wear or carry something bright so people can see you. Take a flashlight.

• Eat only treats that come in store wrappers.

• Visit houses of people you know.

• Walk on sidewalks if you can. Look both ways if you cross a street.

• Try face paint instead of wearing a mask. If you wear a mask, make sure you can see out of it.

• Report any strangers to a grown-up you know. Do not take candy from strangers.

• Trick-or-treat with a grown-up or older sister or brother. Hold hands.

• Stay away from burning jack-o'-lanterns.

Duplicate the list for each child. Children may want to decorate their copies with Halloween stickers or artwork. Send the list home and/or post it.

2. Role-play trick-or-treating. Provide simple costumes. Situations could include:
• "Trick-or-treat" manners—going up to a house (remembering to say "trick-or-treat," "please" and "thank you").
• Crossing a busy street (remembering to "stop, look and listen," and hold hands of older person).
• Being pressured by other children to "trick-or-treat" at a strange house (refusing to participate).

3. Make reflective Halloween bags. Provide small white shopping bags with handles and reflective foil giftwrap or reflective stickers (such as bicycle reflectors) to paste or stick on bags. Children may want to cut Halloween shapes (bats, ghosts, pumpkins, etc.) out of materials. If available, children could also use bright, florescent paint or markers to decorate their bags.

4. Try this safety song (to the tune of "Hot Cross Buns!):
Look both ways.
Look both ways.
When you want to cross the street,
You look both ways.
If you want to get there,
Please make sure that you
stop, look and listen before you
   move!
                  —Laura Alden

More Halloween Fun

1. Things to Create

Make paper bag masks. Provide scissors, paste, felt and fabric scraps (with ric-rac, buttons, ribbons) as well as sequins, pipecleaners and markers. (Or use paints.) Encourage children to invent new Halloween characters such as space aliens or magic monsters.

Make tissue-and-cotton ghosts. For each child, have available cotton ball for head, white tissue to cover ball, orange yarn to tie tissue under ball, black marker to draw face, paste and black paper on which to stick ghost, or more yarn to hang ghosts around room. (For larger puppet ghosts, use white napkin instead of tissue and position a lollipop as head.)

Make paper pumpkin people out of black and orange construction paper. Cut pumpkin as large as orange paper; paste shaped eyes, nose, mouth on both sides of pumpkin. Accordion-fold arms and legs; stick to head. Attach string for hanging.

2. Things to Do

Take turns rolling a ball between two pumpkins. Play "Drop the Witch's Hat" (similar to "Drop the Handkerchief").

3. Things to Share

Learn one or more of the following songs and fingerplays.

Boo-Boo!

(Sung to the tune of Little Green Frog)

Boo-boo went the little white ghost one night,
Boo-boo went the little white ghost.
Boo-boo went the little white ghost one night,
And his friends went boo-boo, too!

Eek-eek went the little brown bat one night,
Eek-eek went the little brown bat.
Eek-eek went the little brown bat one night,
And its friends went eek-eek, too!

Heh-heh went the little black witch one night,
Heh-heh went the little black witch.
Heh-heh went the little black witch one night,
And her friends went heh-heh, too!
—*Laura Alden*

Scary Eyes

I'm a scary ghost.
See my big and scary eyes (circle eyes with thumbs
   and index fingers)?
Look out now for a big surprise—
BOO! (take hands away).

Five Little Pumpkins

Five little pumpkins sitting on a gate.
First one said, "Oh my, it's getting late."
Second one said, "There are witches in the air."
Third one said, "Oh, we don't care."
Fourth one said, "Let's run and run and run."
Fifth one said, "It's Halloween fun."
(Hold hand up and move one finger at a time.)
WOOOOO! went the wind (wave hands).
And out (clap) went the light!
The five little pumpkins rolled out of sight (roll and
   hide hands behind back).

4. Things to Count, Sort and Match

• Sort and count pumpkin faces. Have available several different jack-o'-lantern faces. Color code reverse sides for self-check.

• Set up one-to-one matching activity—hats for witches. Provide a felt board, witches and hats to match.

• Try a touch game. Have available brown bags with Indian corn, a gourd, pumpkin seeds; cut pumpkin, leaves, marshmallows and pictures of these items to match with bag contents. Match by feeling in bag only. Color code bag bottoms and pictures for self-check.

• Create a sequencing and storytelling activity. Provide picture stories to put in sequence.

Examples: Growth of a pumpkin; carving a pumpkin; trick-or-treating; putting on a costume.